# WhenSheepCannotSleep
## THE COUNTING BOOK

# WHEN SHEEP CANNOT SLEEP

## THE COUNTING BOOK

Satoshi Kitamura

RED FOX

Special thanks to Alison Sage for her editorial knitting

A Red Fox Book
Published by Random House Children's Books
20 Vauxhall Bridge Road, London SW1V 2SA
A division of Random House UK Ltd
London  Melbourne  Sydney  Auckland
Johannesburg and agencies throughout the world

First published by A & C Black 1986
Beaver edition 1988
Red Fox edition 1990

9  10

© Satoshi Kitamura 1986

Printed and bound in Italy by
Grafiche, AZ, Verona

Random House UK Limited Reg. No. 954009

ISBN 0 09 950540 1

One night a sheep called Woolly could not sleep.
"I'll go for a walk," he said, and wandered
off down the meadow.

He chased a butterfly until it flew away
behind a tall green tree.

There on the tree trunk were two ladybirds, fast asleep. "I'm still wide awake," thought Woolly.

"Hoo, hoo, hoo," called the owls.
"Time to go home."

"It's *our* time to come out," said a family of bats, flittering overhead.

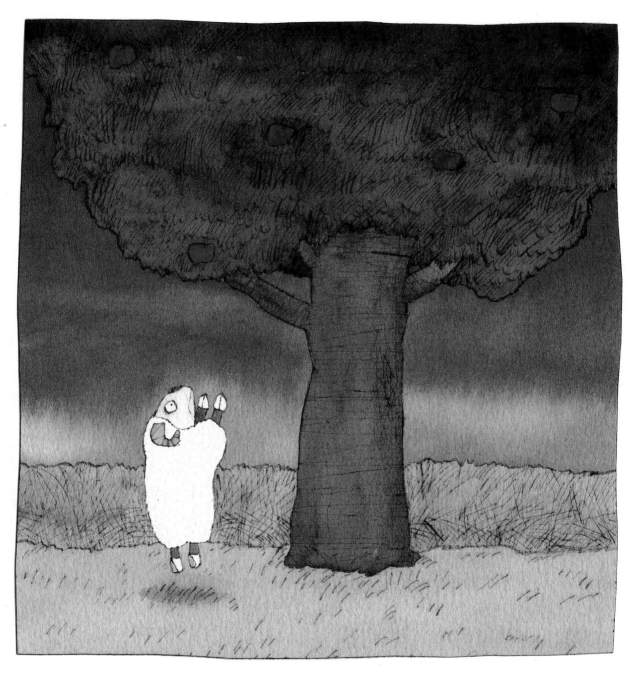

"Apples," said Woolly.
"I knew it was time for something.
    But they are too high up for me."

"Try climbing," said the squirrels.
"Can't," said Woolly.
"There's a ladder," said the squirrels.

They were right.
Woolly put the ladder against the apple tree
and climbed, rung by rung, until he could
reach the sweet, red apples.

It was a lovely calm evening
and Woolly was not a bit sleepy.
Fireflies were dancing in the air . . .

and grasshoppers were singing in the long grass.

Woolly climbed to the top of a hill to look
at the view. Suddenly, flashing lights zipped
across the sky. Woolly was very scared.

He ran as fast as he could to hide
amongst the trees, jumping over red
tulips as he went.

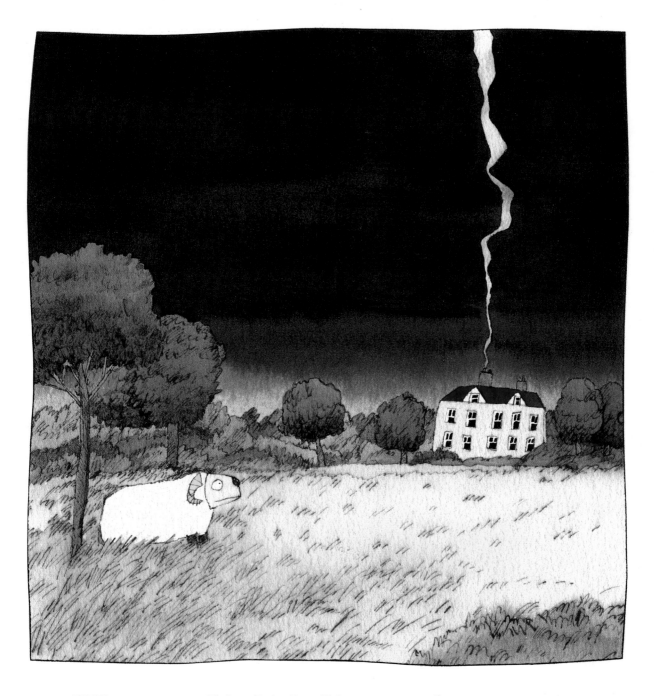

"What a terrible fright," he panted.
"Where am I?" In front of him was a house
with lots of windows.

The front door was open, so he went in.
There were lots of doors, too.

In one of the rooms, he found some
coloured pencils. "Good," said Woolly.
"I'll do some drawing."

He was so pleased with his pictures
that he hung them on the wall.

"I'm hungry again," said Woolly.
He went into the kitchen and cooked himself
some nice green peas.

He took them into the dining room.
"I'm late for supper," he thought.

"Now for a bath," said Woolly,
"with lots of bubbles."

Next door was a little bed, with a pair
of pyjamas laid neatly on it.
"Stars are out already," thought Woolly.

"Perhaps I'll just lie down . . .
    in case I feel sleepy."

He began to think.

He thought about his mother and his father and
his sisters and brothers and uncles and aunts.
What were they doing? Were they already asleep?
His family and friends went round in his head.
His eyes closed.

Woolly was fast asleep.

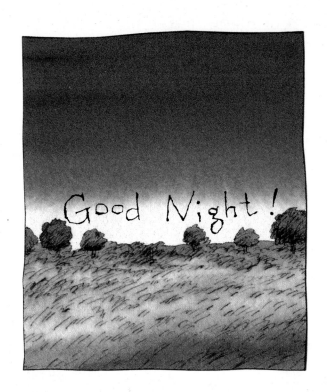

# INDEX

# More Red Fox picture books for you to enjoy